Sinéad Murphy

A TIGER named LEE

Illustrated by

Shannon Cresham

TINY TREE

The jungle is home to such
WONDERFUL CREATURES,
A HAVEN
to those with
the most
VARIED
of features.

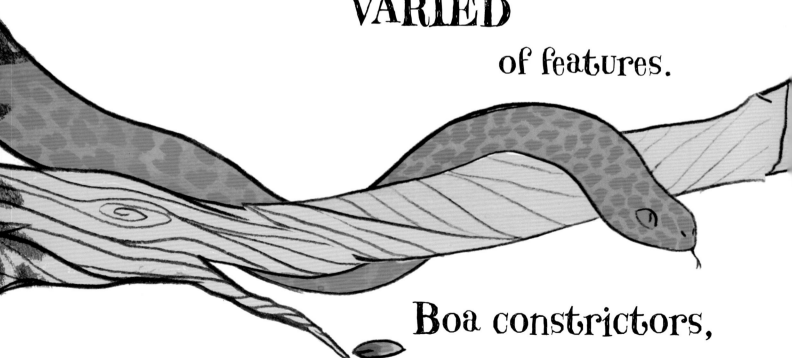

Boa constrictors,

yellow tailed lizards,

Purple nosed monkeys with
strange looking gizzards.

Slithering,

sliding,

JUMPING

and flying.

They spring from the tree
tops without even trying.

A MARVELLOUS realm,
a wonder to see,

It is also the home

of a tiger named

LEE.

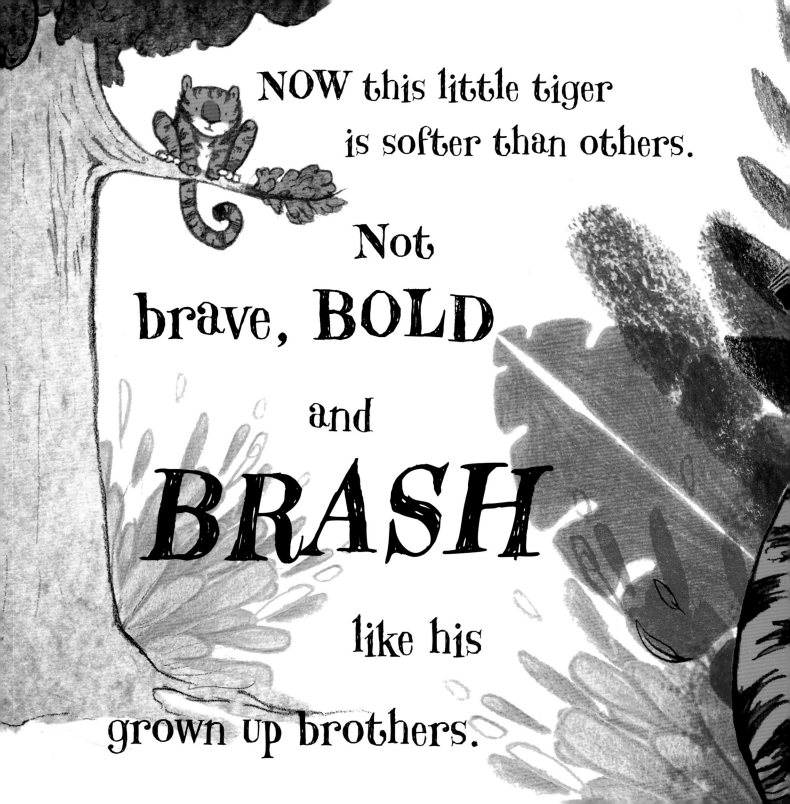

NOW this little tiger
is softer than others.

Not
brave, BOLD
and
BRASH
like his
grown up brothers.

Smaller than most,
he is special you see,

And lives with his Mum
way up high in a tree.

For Lee is a tiger
who refuses to go,

Down from his safe tree
house, to the jungle below.

Who knows of the DANGERS
that await on the floor?

Like

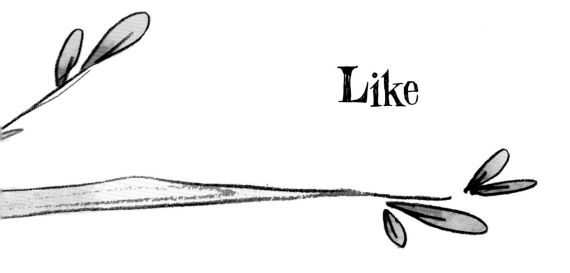

BIG booted
BABOONS

and LIONS
who ROAR.

MOTTLED BACKED GECKOS,
who dart quick as lightening,
Their movement so fast
it's ever so frightening.
Creatures, so fierce and
different from Lee,

He ignores his Mum's calls to,

'COME
DOWN
FROM
THE
TREE!'

Thankfully, Lee's Mum
is patient and kind.

And although he
won't budge,
she just doesn't mind.

She remembers his brothers,
less **BRAVE,**
brash
and

BOLD.

Who had fears of their own,
when they weren't so old.

Wild THUNDER, n' lightning,

and a FOREBODING light.

A

PiERCiNG

LOUD

CRA

CK

A most

frightening

SOUND

And LEE
and his MUM
are thrown
to the GROUND.

They
tumble
and FALL
from way up on HIGH;
and land with a
THUD,

Lee's mum gives a CRY.

Because of their
TERRIBLE
fall from the tree,

She landed quite badly

and has

BROKEN

her knee.

The very next day
all is sunny and clear,
and Lee tries to shake
off his terrible fears.

But out from the bushes
slides a HUGE,
orange,
snake!

Lee squeaks in fright;
he trembles and
SHAKES.

The snake *slithers* closer,
Lee lets out a
YELP,
but the
snake
simply
hisses,
*"May I offer
some help?"*

Lee's mouth falls wide-open at the **SHOCKING** surprise.

The snake isn't scary and has large smiling eyes

Snake gently says "She'll need a strong splint for that, let me call my friend, the **FIERCE** Jaguar Cat."

"**NO!**" Lee blurts out noisily, "He's so terribly **WILD!**"

But Lee's mum assures him, "Don't worry my child."

MR JAGUAR is lovely,
no need for concern,
You have to be BRAVE,
until your
brothers return.'

So, Snake gives a WHISTLE
and word is sent out,
promptly, JAGUAR'S before them
with a SPLINT in his mouth.

Suddenly, so many creatures
are gathered around,
offering help to Lee's
lame mum; who lies
on the ground.

BOA CONSTRICTORS,
yellow tail LIZARDS,

PURPLE
NOSED
MONKEYS
with strange
looking
gizzards.

Lee realises the creatures are
FRIENDLY and **KIND**,
He can't quite believe the change in his mind.

He smiles at the **GECKO**

who offers him water;

And nods to **Ms MONKEY**
as he's introduced to her daughter.

Suddenly this
tiger is feeling
COURAGEOUS,

And does something not
long ago he'd have thought

quite **OUTRAGEOUS!**

Lee steps out alone,
into the jungle so GREEN.

And thrills with surprise
at the things to be seen.

PINK PROWLING PANTHERS
and BOUNCING, BLUE, BUGS.

Lee skips back to his Mummy
for cuddles and hugs.

'MUM you wouldn't believe
all the WONDERS outside!'

Lee's Mum beams with joy
and her heart fills with pride.

'Can you see that your fears
were all in your mind?
And how most of the creatures
are terribly KIND?'

'Yes Mum it's BRILLIANT,
but now I can't be late!
May I join some new friends
for my very first PLAY-DATE?'

Oh, the jungle is home to such
WONDERFUL CREATURES,

A HAVEN

to those with

the most

VARIED

of features.

Each have their own fears and worries you see,

But the one who has conquered his...
Is the **TIGER**
named

LEE!

TINY TREE
CHILDREN'S BOOKS

First Published 2021

Tiny Tree (an imprint of Matthew James Publishing Ltd)

Unit 46, Goyt Mill

Marple

Stockport

SK6 7HX

www.tinytreebooks.co.uk

ISBN: 978-1-910265-89-5

Illustrations by Shannon Cresham